The Chocolate King

'Gam zu l'tovah. Even this is for the good.'
– Nachum Ish Gamzu, Talmud Masechet Taanit, 21a

For chocolate recipes and to learn more
about the history of chocolate, please visit
www.greenbeanbooks.com/chocolate

Green
Bean
Books

APPLES & HONEY PRESS

This edition first published in the UK in 2021 by Green Bean Books
c/o Pen & Sword Books Ltd, 47 Church Street, Barnsley, South Yorkshire, S70 2AS
www.greenbeanbooks.com
Text © Michael Leventhal, 2021 • Illustrations © Laura Catalán, 2021
Chocolate recipe © Claudia Roden, 2012
Copyright © Green Bean Books, 2021 • Hardback edition: 978-1-78438-674-0
Harold Grinspoon Foundation edition: 978-1-7843-8-678-8

Art direction and design by Tina García • Edited by Kate Baker, Julie Carpenter
and Phoebe Jascourt • Production by Hugh Allan
Printed in China   PJ CODE - 0122/B1839/A7

MIX
Paper from
responsible sources
FSC.org
FSC® C020056

Published in North America in 2022 by Apples & Honey Press,
an Imprint of Behrman House Publishers
Millburn, New Jersey 07041
www.applesandhoneypress.com
ISBN 978-1-68115-582-1

Library of Congress Cataloging-in-Publication Data

Names: Leventhal, Michael (Writer on Jewish history), author. | Catalán,
Laura, illustrator. | Roden, Claudia, other.
Title: The Chocolate King / written by Michael Leventhal ;
illustrated by Laura Catalan ; recipe by Claudia Roden.
Description: Millburn, New Jersey : Apples & Honey Press, [2022] |
"First published in the UK in 2021 by Green Bean Books." | Audience: Ages 4-8.
| Audience: Grades K-1. | Summary: In seventeenth-century Spain,
Benjamin and his family leave for France to escape religious
persecution, but in France Benjamin's dreams of making chocolate seem
bleak until a chance encounter with the King of France. Includes a
history of chocolate, the Jewish community, and a recipe for hot chocolate.
Identifiers: LCCN 2021008088 | ISBN 9781681155821 (hardcover)
Subjects: CYAC: Chocolate--Fiction. | Cooking (Chocolate)--Fiction. Jews--France--Fiction.
Classification: LCC PZ7.1.L4859 Ch 2022 | DDC [E]--dc23
LC record available at https://lccn.loc.gov/2021008088

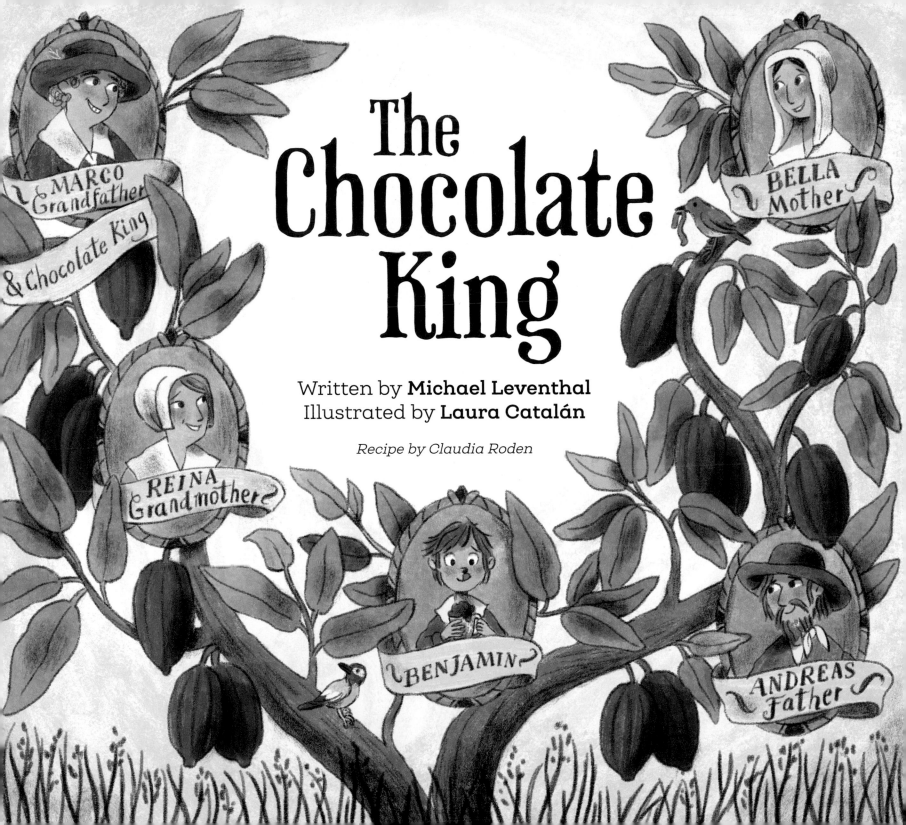

The Chocolate King

Written by **Michael Leventhal**
Illustrated by **Laura Catalán**

Recipe by Claudia Roden

MARCO
Grandfather
& Chocolate King

BELLA
Mother

REINA
Grandmother

BENJAMIN

ANDREAS
Father

Benjamin loved chocolate. He knew more about chocolate than anyone in his town, and more than most people in the whole of France.

But there was one person who knew more than he did – his grandfather, Marco.

Marco made the most incredible
hot chocolate. It was a thick, dark
drink with a crown of foam that
wobbled and stuck to Benjamin's nose.

Benjamin loved sitting with his grandfather and hearing the story of how he had learned to make it.

"It all began in Spain, where we used to live," Marco told Benjamin. "An explorer who visited the faraway lands of America taught me a brilliant Aztec recipe."

"I started selling hot chocolate to rich travelers at the port. I was busy from the minute the sun rose until the last ships sailed out of sight."

"But one day," Marco said sadly, "we heard that the royal court wanted anyone who wasn't Catholic to leave the country – including Jewish people like us.

We stayed in Spain for as long as we could, but finally we had to leave.

We packed as much as possible and left late one night. You were only a baby, Benjamin," he said.

"We took as many cocoa beans as we could carry.
Your mother said clothes were more useful, but
I insisted that the beans were our family's treasure!"

"When we arrived here in France, no one had ever seen or tried hot chocolate," Marco continued. "I wanted us to be the first to show them how wonderful it tastes."

"Your father wasn't happy. He said people don't like trying new things and they wouldn't want our chocolate."

"But I was determined!
Besides, making chocolate was
the only skill I had. And that's
how we started our life here."

As Benjamin grew older, he wanted to help make the chocolate – but Marco would only let him watch, listen, and smell. Marco was strict with everyone!

Benjamin's grandma, Reina, showed him how to grind the roasted cocoa beans, but he was never allowed to touch.

Every night, Benjamin went to bed dreaming of becoming a Chocolate King too.

Marco and his family were very good at making chocolate, but Benjamin's father had been right. Very few people wanted to buy it.

Chocolate was expensive – and even those who could afford it thought it was strange.

"Not for me!"

"It's great!"

"That's the worst glop I've ever seen!"

"It looks like sticky mud."

So, like most other Jewish people who lived in their town, Marco's family struggled to make money.

"I might be the Chocolate King, but I'm the poorest king that France has ever seen!" Marco sighed.

Then, one morning, something
extraordinary happened.

Benjamin tried to sneak into the kitchen
to watch his family at work – but his
mother spotted him.
"Get on with your chores!" she said.
"I want to watch Grandpa,"
he protested.

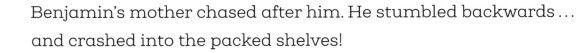

Benjamin's mother chased after him. He stumbled backwards…
and crashed into the packed shelves!

Plates, pans, cans, and jars clattered to the floor. A large pot
filled with thick chocolate toppled over – and emptied all over
Benjamin! It covered his hair, dribbled onto his face, and
trickled down his back.

Benjamin tumbled out of the kitchen and onto the cobbled street, straight into the path of a gleaming, golden carriage.

"What on earth is that creature
caked in mud?" demanded
an angry passenger.

"It isn't mud – it's chocolate!" protested Benjamin.
"My grandpa is the Chocolate King!"

There was a pause.
And then the carriage door flew open
and a podgy, pink-faced man stepped out.

"Really?" he asked. "I thought I was the only king here!"

"Your M-M-Majesty," stammered Benjamin.

"I'm so sorry. I-I-I had no idea!"

The King of France inspected Benjamin from head to toe. And then the smell of chocolate slowly drifted to his nostrils, and a smile spread across his face.

"Well, I must confess something does smell rather appealing. Let me taste this chocolate."

Marco hurriedly prepared a cup of the family's finest hot chocolate, topped with a crown of wobbling foam. He rushed out of the house, covered in cocoa dust, and gingerly approached the royal carriage. He presented the cup to the king.

The king took a sip, then another, and then he gulped the rest down. He passed the cup back to Marco and asked for more.

Finally, four cups later, he pulled out a large, silk handkerchief and wiped his mouth clean. Then he let out an enormous burp.

Burrrrrrrrrrrrrrrrrrp!

"This chocolate is divine," he said. "I'll have ten flasks, please, and I'll pay you handsomely."

Benjamin danced around the kitchen punching the air, while his grandpa was too shocked to move. His mother lifted his father into the air!

"Benjamin, your chocolate catastrophe has worked a miracle!" Marco told his grandson. "Now that we have royal approval, we'll be famous throughout France!"

Marco was right. Soon, there were lines of customers eager to try the new drink. Orders began arriving from every corner of the country.

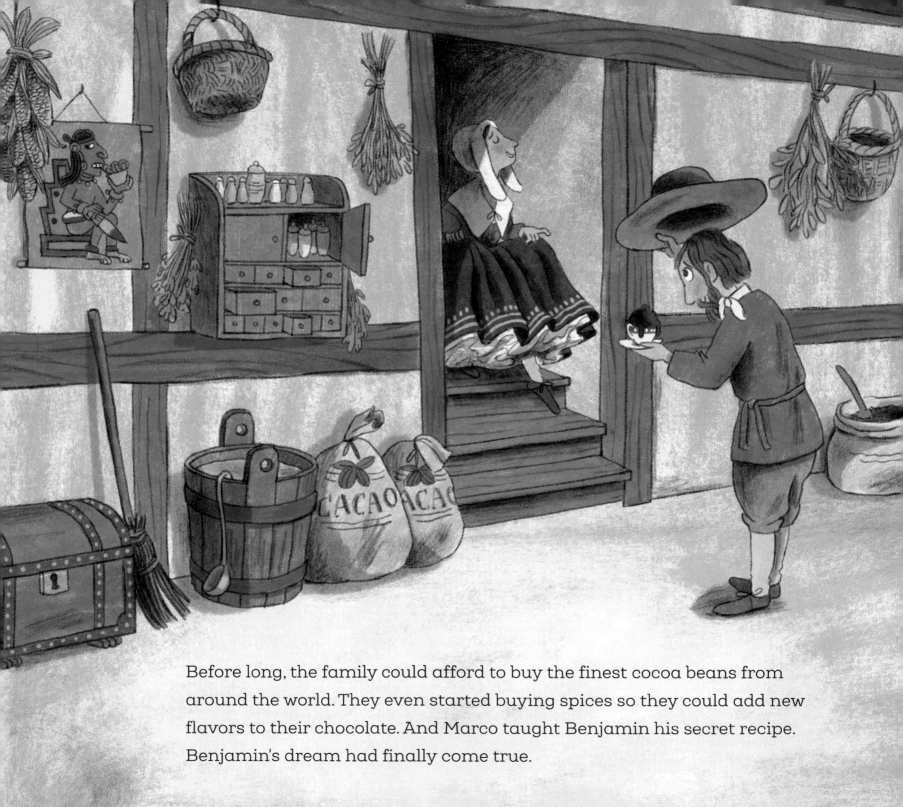

Before long, the family could afford to buy the finest cocoa beans from around the world. They even started buying spices so they could add new flavors to their chocolate. And Marco taught Benjamin his secret recipe. Benjamin's dream had finally come true.

A Bite-Sized History of Chocolate

and the Jewish Community

Circa 600 The Maya develop a chocolate drink called *kawkaw* that they mix with spices and water.

1478 The Spanish Inquisition begins, forcing thousands of Jews to leave Spain or live as *conversos.*

* A converso was a Jew who converted to Catholicism.

1521 The Aztecs initially welcome the Spanish, but Cortés later takes Montezuma hostage, and battles break out. After fierce fighting, the Spanish overpower the Aztecs and seize control. Treasured Aztec *chocolatl* is taken back to Spain.

1580 Spain begins regular imports of cocoa beans, and a chocolate industry develops.

1519 Don Hernán Cortés becomes the first European to taste *chocolatl* in the court of the Aztec emperor, Montezuma.

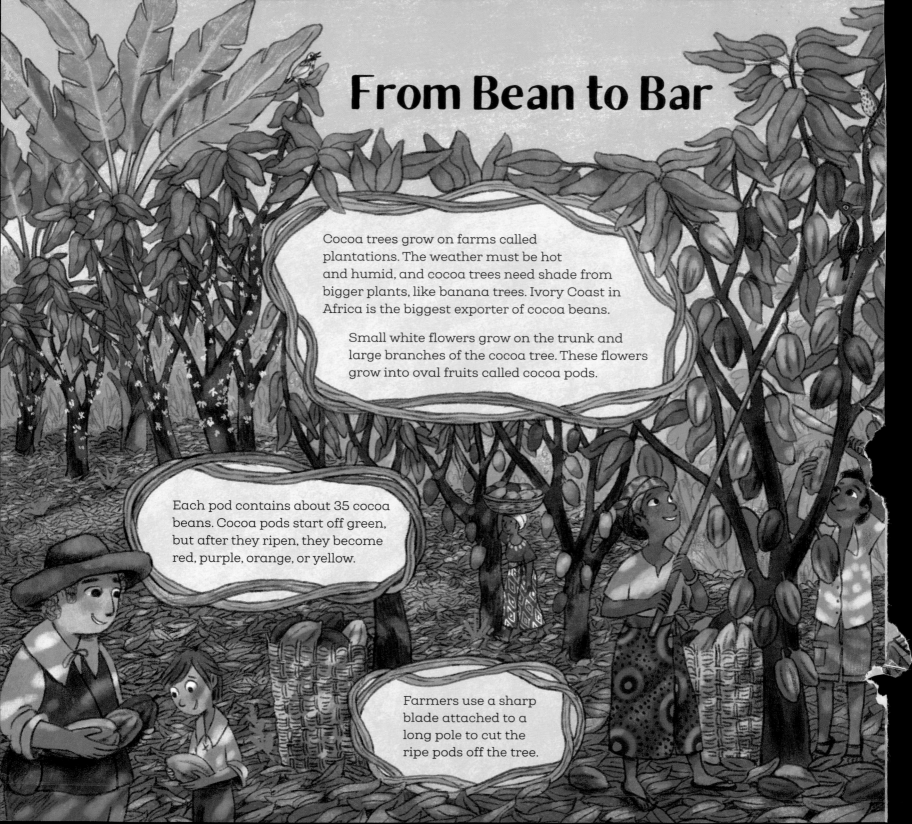

From Bean to Bar

Cocoa trees grow on farms called plantations. The weather must be hot and humid, and cocoa trees need shade from bigger plants, like banana trees. Ivory Coast in Africa is the biggest exporter of cocoa beans.

Small white flowers grow on the trunk and large branches of the cocoa tree. These flowers grow into oval fruits called cocoa pods.

Each pod contains about 35 cocoa beans. Cocoa pods start off green, but after they ripen, they become red, purple, orange, or yellow.

Farmers use a sharp blade attached to a long pole to cut the ripe pods off the tree.

The pods are opened, and the beans and pulp are removed. The beans are put in heaps on the floor, covered with banana leaves, then left to ferment – or break down – for a few days. The temperature rises until the sugar in the pulp drains away.

The fermentation process mellows the natural bitterness of the cocoa beans. It actually changes the sugar to acid.

The beans are spread out to dry in the sun. Once dry, some of the beans are packed and sent to factories around the world.

There, the beans are roasted at a high temperature to improve the flavor.

Every day, as he helped to make the thick, dark drink with a crown of wobbly foam, Benjamin would proudly declare:

"Now I am a Chocolate King too!"

Author

Michael Leventhal is the publisher of Green Bean Books. *The Chocolate King* is his first children's book and won a PJ Library Author Incentive Award. He was the founder of the Jewish food charity Gefiltefest and was co-author of *Jews in Britain*. He eats a lot of chocolate and compiled a collection of chocolate recipes called *Babka, Boulou & Blintzes*. www.michaelleventhal.co.uk.

Dedicated to Rachel, Sammy and Jack.

Illustrator

Laura Catalán is a Spanish children's books illustrator currently based in Barcelona. After studying anthropology, she spent years attending drawing lessons and illustration courses in the Cercle Artistic Sant LLuç in Barcelona, before starting her professional career as an illustrator. Since then, she has published numerous educational materials, middle-grade books and picture books for Spanish, UK and USA publishers. www.lauracatalan.com

Dedicated to María and Sesé.

Thanks to:

Kate Baker

Nicola Christie

Jill Burrows

Julie Carpenter

Claire Berliner

Tina García

Helen Guthrie

Susannah Okret

Ursula Milton

Simon Rosenberg

Phoebe Jascourt

Thick Hot Chocolate Drink

Chocolate a la taza by Claudia Roden

Thick, creamy, rich hot chocolate served with *churros* (long, ribbed, crisp dough fritters) is a popular breakfast in Spain. *Chocolaterías* specialize in the drink, which is made with dark bitter chocolate and a little cornflour to thicken the milk. The amount of sugar needed depends on the sweetness of the chocolate.

Ingredients
(Serves 2)

- 2 teaspoons cornflour (corn starch)
- 500ml (2 cups) whole milk
- 100g (4 ounces) grated dark chocolate
- 2–3 teaspoons sugar, or to taste

Instructions

1 Dissolve the cornflour in 2 tablespoons of cold milk.

2 Bring the rest of the milk to the boil in a saucepan and pour in the cornflour mixture, stirring with a wooden spoon.

3 Cook over a low heat for 2 to 3 minutes, stirring until the milk thickens slightly and becomes creamy.

4 Add the chocolate and keep stirring until it has melted entirely. Then stir in the sugar to taste.

1630 A survey estimates that there are 60 Jewish *converso* families living in Saint Esprit, outside Bayonne, France.

This is the time and place where Marco and Benjamin's story is set.

1650 Jacob the Jew opens England's first coffeehouse, The Angel, in Oxford, where he serves both coffee and hot chocolate.

1663 Jewish chocolatier Emmanuel Soares de Rinero begins making chocolate in Belgium.

1701 The chocolate trade to New York begins, with beans imported from the Caribbean by Jewish trader Isaac Marquez.

1830s Pastry chef Franz Sacher, who many people believe was Jewish, creates chocolate Sachertorte for Austria's Prince Metternich.

Eventually, chocolatiers start making solid bars of chocolate. And today, Bayonne boasts chocolate shops, museums, and an annual chocolate festival.